Lester's Dog

For the whole West Garrison Avenue gang
but especially for Joey— K.H.

For Jill—N.C.

Text copyright © 1993 by Karen Hesse
Illustrations copyright © 1993 by Nancy Carpenter
Published by Crown Publishers, Inc., a Random House company,
 201 East 50th Street, New York, New York 10022
CROWN is a trademark of Crown Publishers, Inc.
Manufactured in Singapore

Library of Congress Cataloging-in-Publication Data
Hesse, Karen.
Lester's dog / by Karen Hesse ; illustrated by Nancy Carpenter.
 p. cm.
Summary: A boy overcomes his fear of Lester's fierce dog
when he has to protect an abandoned kitten.
[1. Dogs —Fiction. 2. Fear — Fiction.] I. Carpenter, Nancy, ill. II. Title.
PZ7.H4364Ld 1993
[E] — dc20   92-27674

ISBN 0-517-58357-7 (trade)
        0-517-58358-5 (lib. bdg.)

10 9 8 7 6 5 4 3 2 1   FIRST EDITION

LESTER'S DOG

by **Karen Hesse**   illustrated by **Nancy Carpenter**

CROWN PUBLISHERS, INC.   New York

On long summer days, Mama scoots me out of the house after dinner. Same as always, I sit on the front stoop, watching robins rake the grass for worms, and wait for Corey to come out.

An old Chevy slides around the corner and, gears grinding, climbs up the hill. Just before the car drops down the back side of Garrison Avenue, Lester's dog tears out from under his porch and lunges at the car's wheels. You can hear him barking clear to the end of the block. He swaggers back when the car is gone and hunkers down under his porch again. I shiver, touching the scar on my nose where Lester's dog bit me when I was six.

I'm busy wishing bad things on Lester's dog when Corey comes up beside me, sticks out his hand, and pulls me off the stoop. He's tugging like he wants me to follow him up the hill, to the top of Garrison Avenue.

I shake my head. "I'm not going past Lester's dog tonight," I say. But Corey's bigger than I am, and he steers me up the hill anyway. It doesn't matter what you say to Corey, 'cause he can't hear you, and even if he could, he's too stubborn to listen.

We pass Corey's house first, and then Mr. Frank's. I sort of count on Mr. Frank always being there, sitting in his big chair, looking out over the block. Mama says he's a broken man since Mrs. Frank died, and I've been wondering for some time now just what it'd take to fix him.

I wave to him and he nods back. That's our way of talking, me and Mr. Frank.

We're almost at Lester's house now, its lawn all patched and dusty, and the grass gone from Lester's dog digging it up. I'm so scared of that dog the hair's standing up on my arms and down my spine. I try pulling Corey back the way we came, but nothing stops Corey, not even Lester's dog.

I pick up a stone and squeeze it in my fist. But even I know a little stone won't scare Lester's dog.

Corey gazes into the shadows under Lester's porch. Then he takes my hand and walks me straight past Lester's house.

I feel my heart squeezing up in my throat and my legs ready to run, but Lester's dog is too busy digging dust under his porch to notice me and Corey. Before I know it, we're past him, standing at the top of Garrison Avenue.

We look back, but Lester's dog is still under his porch, chewing dirt. I grin at Corey. "We made it," I say, swinging his hand. And Corey grins back.

We walk down the hill on our toes to keep from going too fast. At the corner of Garrison and Pimlico, Corey gears up to cross the road. Traffic roars past, whipping up licks of my shirt that are not stuck down with sweat. I squeeze Corey's hand hard and he frowns, his head swiveling back and forth, back and forth, waiting for a good time to cross. And then there's a break in the traffic, and Corey pulls me off the curb. We fly over Pimlico Road like Lester's dog is chasing us.

Safely on the other side, Corey pulls me toward an old building. He stops at a wooden bulkhead.

"You brought me past Lester's dog for this?" I ask, squinting up into Corey's face. But then I hear something crying, and it's coming from beneath the bulkhead door.

Corey stoops down close to the pavement. The handle to the door is broken off, so he curls his fingers around the splintery edge and lifts it over his head. I shift back and forth from one foot to the other, trying to look past Corey into the shadows of the cellar way.

Then, on the steps, I see a tiny fist of fur, knotted up. I hear it mewing, mewing like a stuck record. Corey reaches in and scoops up a single kitten. He cups it to his ear like he was listening to the sea. One skinny paw catches in the wire of Corey's hearing aid but Corey doesn't mind. He just holds that kitten to his ear, listening.

I touch Corey's shoulder, and he looks at me real serious, then eases the kitten into my hands. I feel ribs and bones jutting up under scraggly fur. The kitten wriggles and turns in my fingers. It sucks at my sweaty shirt.

Corey lowers the wooden door and motions me to follow him back home.

"We can't take this kitten," I say. "If we take it, we've got to care for it."

But Corey doesn't hear, and even if he does I'm not saying anything he doesn't already know. I try to open the bulkhead myself to put the kitten back, but Corey stamps his foot down on the wooden door. He takes me by my elbow, leads me to the curb, and with his fingers clamped on to me and me clamped on to that kitten, we tear back across Pimlico Road.

The kitten mews and mews in my hands. I tuck it under my shirt so it will stop shivering. Its rough tongue scrubs the same spot on my stomach till it drives me crazy. I slip the kitten back out and hold it up close to my face.

"What are we going to do with you?" I ask. "I sure can't keep you. Mama says cats make her itch." The kitten's head tips to one side like it's listening to me, and I rub its fur against my cheek.

Before I know it, we're at the top of Garrison Avenue. And there, two lawns down, is Lester's dog, staring up at us and waiting.

Corey tries taking my hand, but my hands are full of kitten. So he starts down the hill first, looking straight ahead, and I follow.

Corey gets by all right and keeps going down the hill, but Lester's dog growls at me. He growls low and nasty. My legs feel like they're dragging bricks. The kitten starts mewing and shivering worse than ever.

For a second, everything is frozen like that—Corey almost home, and me staring at Lester's dog, and Lester's dog staring back. And then Lester's dog comes unstuck, and he springs at me like I was some old Chevy.

I run, holding tight to the kitten, and Lester's dog snaps and snarls at my heels.

I am halfway down the hill, almost to Mr. Frank's, when I feel Lester's dog slap my back with his paws. My head whips around, and I struggle to stay on my feet.

Lester's dog leaps up, barking and snapping, his eyes locked on the kitten. I lift the kitten higher, but Lester's dog grabs at my shirt, ripping it with his teeth.

All the times I've been scared is all bundled into right now. But suddenly what I'm feeling is not scared. What I'm feeling is mad!

A rumbling starts deep in my throat. I glare into that dog's face, and a sound rises up from a place inside of me I didn't know was there. My whole body fills with the sound and the ground seems to shake under me as I roar at Lester's dog.

And then Lester's dog is backing off. He's leaving, whining and slinking all the way up the block, crawling on his belly to hide under Lester's porch.

All of me is trembling, and my legs feel like loose Jell-O. I sit down on the curb waiting for the shaking to pass, holding tight to the kitten.

When I look up, Corey is beside me, gazing over his shoulder toward Mr. Frank's house. But Mr. Frank isn't in his chair anymore. He's standing on the porch and he's waving. I look at Corey and I know just what to do with that kitten after all.

Walking up the swept path, I reach out to Mr. Frank.

"Here, Mr. Frank," I say, pressing the kitten into his open hands.

Mr. Frank stands by the porch rail. He doesn't call after me. He doesn't ask any questions. He just stands there talking baby talk to that scrawny kitten.

Corey lays his arm across my shoulder and I reach up and lay my arm across his. We walk down the street and settle ourselves on my stoop.

I sit with Corey like that, slapping mosquitoes and watching while cars climb up the hill past Lester's house and drop home free down the other side, till Mama calls me in.